ILLIS HOLT

PiPER REED
RoDeo StaR

Illustrated by
CHRISTINE DAVENIER

HENRY HOLT AND COMPANY

NEW YORK

SQUARE
FISH

An Imprint of Macmillan

PIPER REED, RODEO STAR. Text copyright © 2011 by Kimberly Willis Holt.
Illustrations copyright © 2011 by Christine Davenier.
All rights reserved. Printed in the United States of America by
R. R. Donnelley & Sons Company, Harrisonburg, Virginia. For information, address
Square Fish, 175 Fifth Avenue, New York, NY 10010.

Square Fish and the Square Fish logo are trademarks of Macmillan and
are used by Henry Holt and Company under license from Macmillan.

Library of Congress Cataloging-in-Publication Data
Holt, Kimberly Willis.
Piper Reed, rodeo star / Kimberly Willis Holt ; illustrated by Christine Davenier.
p. cm.
"Christy Ottaviano Books."
Summary: After bidding goodbye to her friends Michael and Nicole, who are moving away,
Piper and her sisters spend winter break with their two sets of grandparents in Piney Woods,
Louisiana, where Piper learns that the best adventures are the unexpected ones.
ISBN 978-1-250-00409-3
[1. Family life—Louisiana—Fiction. 2. Sisters—Fiction. 3. Grandparents—Fiction. 4. Christmas—Fiction.
5. United States. Navy—Fiction. 6. Louisiana—Fiction.] I. Davenier, Christine, ill. II. Title.
PZ7.H74023Pir 2011 [Fic]—dc22 2010032879

Originally published in the United States by
Christy Ottaviano Books/Henry Holt and Company
First Square Fish Edition: August 2012
Square Fish logo designed by Filomena Tuosto
mackids.com

1 3 5 7 9 10 8 6 4 2

AR: 3.6 / LEXILE: 580L

For my cousins, who knew adventures could be found in small places, Sherri Willis Cormier, Marella Willis Hubachek, Aline Willis Lowe, Donna Mizell Smith, Mitchell Mizell, and Sandie Butter Rollins, and in memory of Donald Willis Jr. and David Willis

Piper Reed
Rodeo Star

CONTENTS

1

A PINEY WOODS CHRISTMAS

Mom and Chief were going on a honeymoon to Paris, France. Chief called it a second honeymoon, but Mom said she didn't call driving from Piney Woods, Louisiana, to Waukegan, Illinois, in an old Buick Impala a honeymoon. Mom and Chief lived in Waukegan when Chief received his first assignment at the Great Lakes Naval Station.

"Where will we stay while you're in France?" I asked.

"Piney Woods," said Chief. "You girls can have a nice visit with your grandparents."

Both sets of our grandparents lived in the country. And they both had a few animals—not enough to be a real farm, but it was the closest to a farm that we'd ever seen.

We were sitting on the back porch while Chief barbecued chicken on the grill. Bruna ran around the yard, barking. Anytime we gathered out in the backyard Bruna got excited, as if the yard belonged to her and we were her guests.

"What about Bruna?" I asked.

Chief snapped the tongs three times before using them to turn the chicken. "She can go, too," he said. "Although you'll have to keep her on a leash when she's outside. Remember what happened when we took her camping, Piper?"

I didn't need to be reminded. It had been my fault when Bruna wandered off Halloween night and caused us to form a search party.

"How about Peaches the Second?" Sam asked. "Can she go to Piney Woods?"

"Brady's family will watch your goldfish," Mom said. "Piney Woods is too far of a drive for Peaches."

"Peaches *the Second*," said Sam. "But who will feed her?"

"We've already asked Yolanda. She said Brady would love to take care of your fish."

Sam folded her arms in front of her chest. "Brady is too little."

"What's the big deal?" I asked. "It's just sprinkling fish flakes in the fishbowl."

Tori sighed. "I've always wanted to go to France." My big sister thought she should get to do anything she wanted since she was thirteen years old.

I told her, "Tori, you just think France has a huge all-you-can-eat buffet with french fries." She loved french fries and just about any other thing called food.

"That's not why!" Tori snapped. "I want to see the Eiffel Tower and the Louvre. I want to walk the streets of Montmartre where van Gogh lived."

Sam jumped to her feet. "I know who Vincent van Gogh is." My little sister was the

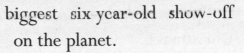

biggest six year-old show-off on the planet.

"We all know van Gogh," I said. Mom was our art teacher at school, but even before that, she made sure we knew every great master. Anytime a museum had a special exhibit, Mom acted as if it was a new roller-coaster ride at Six Flags and took us. I actually liked going to the museum exhibits. But not as much as I wanted to ride a roller coaster.

"Just think of the fun you'll have with all your relatives," Mom said. "And your grandparents are looking forward to spending time with you."

"When are you leaving?" I asked.

"During the holidays," Mom said. "We'll be back in time to ring in the new year."

Sam's eyes bulged. "You won't be with us for Christmas?"

Mom looked at Chief, who cleared his throat and said, "I'm sorry, girls. There was no other way. You get out a few days before Christmas, and I couldn't get off sooner than that."

Mom held the platter for Chief while he removed the chicken from the grill. I loved Chief's barbecued chicken because of the secret ingredient (Louisiana hot sauce!).

"Tori," Chief said, "please set the picnic table."

"It's Piper's turn," Tori snapped.

"Piper?" Chief said.

I saluted him. "Aye, aye, Chief." I dashed into the house and opened the silverware drawer. I was going to miss Mom and Chief. Last year Chief was on a ship during Christmas, but we'd never spent Christmas without Mom.

When I came back out, I studied all the sad

faces around the table. The USS *Reed Family* ship was sinking fast. Somebody had to cheer up the crew. I decided to start with the squirt. "Don't worry, Sam. Santa can figure out where you are."

Little puddles filled Sam's eyes. "Who will read us *The Night Before Christmas*?"

Every Christmas Eve, Chief read *Cajun Night Before Christmas*, which is kind of like the regular *Night Before Christmas*, only it has alligators instead of reindeer and gumbo instead of sugarplums.

No one said anything. Sam stared my way. "Don't look at me!" I snapped. Except for dog books like *Shiloh* and *Sable*, I'd rather go to the mall all day with Tori than read. Even if I didn't have dyslexia, I'd find something else to do.

"I'll read it," Tori said. That figured. She would probably require a costume and make us pay admission to listen to her read.

"Chicken's ready," Chief said. We settled around the picnic table. Smoke from the grill was dying down, and the smell of our chicken mixed with other barbecue smells from our neighbors' backyards in the enlisted housing. That's what was nice about living in Florida. You could barbecue all year long.

Chief passed the bowl of potato salad. "Girls, this was a hard decision for us to make. We hate missing Christmas, but your mom and I haven't had any time by ourselves since before Tori was born. Sometimes parents need a little alone time."

"Why?" I asked. "Aren't we any fun?"

Mom looked at Chief. "Karl, this is starting to feel like a terrible idea. Maybe we could wait until another year."

"When?" Chief asked. "When all the girls are grown?"

"Hey," I said, "great idea!"

Chief frowned at me.

"Bad idea," I mumbled.

Chief shook his head. "Edie, we'll lose the deposit money."

All of a sudden, I felt torn down the middle. I wanted them to stay. I wanted them to go.

Then I heard myself say, "Mom, you and Chief go to Paris. Sometimes kids need a little alone time without parents."

2

~~~

MUTINY ON THE PLAYGROUND

In a few days we would be on winter break. Then we'd drive to the Alexandria Airport. Before Mom and Chief got on a plane to Paris, our grandparents would meet us.

Mom had always wanted to go to Paris, even before she took Swoosie's class at college. She told us, "When I was a little girl, I checked out a book from the library about France. I fell in love with those pictures. I even resorted to lying, telling my parents I'd lost the book. Momma found it under my bed, and I got punished for lying. But I checked out that book again and again."

It was hard to picture Mom as a little girl or lying. I would never lie about a book, but once I lied about doing my homework. Well, maybe more than once. I guess it's in my genes.

The week before the holidays, I was standing near the flagpole with the other Gypsy Club members. We were talking about what gifts we hoped to get for Christmas.

"I don't get gifts for Christmas," Stanley said.

"You don't?" Nicole asked.

"No," he said. "But I do for Hanukkah."

I couldn't believe he hadn't told us that yet.

Even though Stanley was the newest member of our club, we knew the most about him. Because he was such a blabbermouth.

Michael interrupted. "I need to call an emergency meeting. Let's meet back here at recess."

No one had ever announced an emergency meeting except for me. It kind of caught me by surprise, and I said, "You can't call an emergency Gypsy Club meeting."

"Why not?" Michael asked.

"Because I started the Gypsy Club. Only I can call emergency meetings."

Hailey slapped her hands on her hips. "Who made up that dumb rule?" she said as she turned away and kicked at a pebble.

Stanley pushed at the bridge of his glasses. "I didn't know that rule, and I thought you had told me all of them. There's the rule about having to be a military brat and the rule about living in at least three places and the rule about—"

Once Stanley Hampshire started talking, he wouldn't quit. He moved from topic to topic like a Ping-Pong ball bouncing over a net in an Olympic competition.

"Stop, Stanley!" I said, holding up the palm of my hand.

He shut up.

I sighed. "I motion that Michael can call an emergency Gypsy Club meeting."

"*Just* Michael?" Hailey said. "Well, I motion that *any* member can call an emergency Gypsy Club meeting."

Oh brother! This was starting to feel like a mutiny. "*Any* member?"

Then every member, except Nicole, who was staring at the clouds, shouted, "Anyone!"

Michael groaned when he realized Nicole hadn't joined in. It was hard to believe he and Nicole were twins.

"Well . . . we have to make it official," Nicole said.

Hailey walked back over and blurted out, "I motion that ANY member of the Gypsy Club—"

The school bell rang. We'd have to finish being official at recess.

3
~~~
MICHAEL AND NICOLE'S
BIG SURPRISE

All morning I couldn't concentrate at school. My mind was busy wondering why Michael needed to call an emergency meeting. Maybe Michael wanted to plan a wonderful Gypsy Club adventure during the holidays, something I wouldn't be able to do because I'd be in Piney Woods.

Maybe he was going to plan a day cruise on a boat. But Michael's family didn't have a boat. Stanley's dad did. Maybe he was going to invite everyone to a cookout at Pensacola Beach. Or maybe he was going to suggest we break a roller-coaster riding record. I read that someone rode a roller coaster for more than 120 hours. Since we had all that time off, we could ride for days. I could see the headlines—GYPSY CLUB MEMBERS BREAK WORLD ROLLER-COASTER RIDING RECORD. Only I wouldn't be a part of it. I'd be in Piney Woods. Now spending the holidays in Piney Woods didn't seem like fun. Then I decided I would have my own adventure. But just one? How about two? Or three? No. I would have *four* great adventures.

During class I studied Michael, searching for a hint, but he never glanced my way. Finally the bell rang and I sprang from my seat. I raced out the front door and headed toward the flagpole. I wanted to be the first to hear Michael's announcement. Halfway there, I realized I'd left Michael behind. Soon I saw him and Stanley making their way toward me.

"Okay, why did you call the emergency meeting?" I asked.

"I can't tell you yet," Michael said. "Everyone isn't here."

It seemed like I was losing my special privileges by the minute.

"Besides, it's also Nicole's news," Michael said.

Nicole's news, too? Michael and Nicole had a surprise. What could it be? Maybe Michael and Nicole were going to get a new baby brother or sister. I could tell them all about how lousy it would be with a baby in the house, a baby that gets all the attention and becomes a spelling bee prodigy.

Hailey and Nicole rushed up to the flagpole.

"Well?" Hailey said.

"Wait!" Nicole said, like she'd forgotten something important.

"What?" I asked.

"We forgot to make it official," she said. Leave it to Nicole to remind us about the rules.

I sighed. "Hailey, take up where you left off."

"I motion that ANY Gypsy Club member can call an emergency meeting." Hailey glared

at me when she said *ANY*. "All in favor?"

Everyone but me said, "Aye!"

"Wait!" I said.

Michael's tongue made a snapping sound. "What now?"

"I think we should have some guidelines on what is important enough to call an emergency meeting."

"Trust me, Piper," Michael said. "*This* is important enough."

I looked to Nicole. She nodded.

"Well?" Hailey said, waiting.

"Aye," I softly said.

"All opposed?" Hailey asked.

Silence.

I twisted around, facing Michael. "Okay, what's so important?"

Michael took a deep breath. "Nicole and I are moving."

No one spoke. Nicole looked like she was going to cry. I would miss her. Nicole never got mad at anyone, no matter what they said or did. But I would miss Michael the most. He was my best friend. He could touch his nose with his tongue and turn an okay time into a "get off the bus!" day.

Now I would be stuck with Hailey, who thought she knew everything, and Stanley, who didn't know when to shut up.

"Why do you have to move?" I asked.

"Hello, Piper?" Michael said. "Our mom is in the Navy."

"I guess for a minute I forgot."

"Where are you moving?" asked Hailey.

"Norfolk," Nicole said.

"Norfolk, Virginia?" Stanley asked.

Michael rolled his eyes. "Is there any other Norfolk with a Navy base?"

"Well, as you may remember," Stanley said,

"I lived in Norfolk, Virginia. I can tell you all about it. You can visit a lot of neat historical places nearby. There's Jamestown, Monticello, Williamsburg . . ."

On and on Stanley went about living in Virginia and all someone could do there. You would have thought he was a travel agent.

Finally Stanley finished by saying, "And you can visit my grandparents."

Michael wrinkled his forehead. "Your grandparents?"

"Yep," Stanley said. "My grandfather was an admiral, and he retired in Virginia Beach. That's close to Norfolk."

"I'd like to meet your grandparents," Nicole said. "Our grandparents are dead."

I was lucky. My four grandparents were alive and well in Piney Woods. But all I could think about was what my life would be like without Michael and Nicole.

4

GOING-AWAY PARTY

Friday night was the going-away party for Michael and Nicole's family. Saturday they would leave for Norfolk. Sunday we'd be leaving for Piney Woods. I didn't want to go to the party. The party meant having to say goodbye. Somehow not going made me think that Michael and Nicole wouldn't be leaving. But that was silly. Michael and Nicole would be leaving whether or not I went to the party.

At school Ms. Gordon made an announcement. "Class, today is Michael's last day with us. His family is moving to Norfolk, Virginia. How many of you have lived in Norfolk?"

Eight classmates, including Stanley, raised their hands.

"Well," she said, "then make sure you tell Michael something wonderful about living there before class ends."

Stanley jumped to his feet. "I can tell Michael all about Norfolk," he said, as if he hadn't already been cramming Michael's head with facts about the city.

"Not now, Stanley," Ms. Gordon said. Her right eye began to twitch.

Stanley sank back into his seat.

Throughout the day, those eight classmates came up to Michael and told him what to expect in Norfolk.

Kelsey, who had never wanted to sit with any of the Gypsy Club members, squeezed between Michael and me at lunch and said, "It snows there in the winter."

Jacob plopped across from Michael. "Virginia Beach is nearby," he said. "You can have a lot of fun there in the summer."

"And my grandparents live there," Stanley added for the eighteenth time.

"You can ride a paddleboat ferry downtown," Matthew told Michael at recess. "Hey, you want to play tetherball? I'll tell you the names of my friends who still live there."

Michael took off with Matthew, leaving me alone with Stanley, Nicole, and Hailey. I took a bite of my peanut butter and honey sandwich. It tasted bland like paper.

After school, I waited for Mom and Sam while Stanley walked away with Michael, telling him about how he could get a parrot in Norfolk. "They have a pet store with just birds. I guess it's really a bird store."

"Well, I doubt we'll get a parrot," Michael said. "Nicole is allergic to birds."

My last day of school, and I hadn't had one spare minute with Michael.

At home, Sam was already packing her suitcase for our visit to Piney Woods. We weren't going for two days. Why was everyone in such a hurry to leave Pensacola?

Sam was trying to decide if she wanted to

bring her doll Annie with her. Three times, she'd packed Annie in the suitcase, and three times she'd pulled her out.

"Don't forget," I told her. "It gets really dark in the country. They don't have any street-lights."

Sam frowned at me. "So?" But when she thought I wasn't looking, I saw her slip Annie into her suitcase before slapping the lid shut.

A few minutes later, Mom hollered up, "To-ri! Pi-per! Sam! It's time to go to the party!"

Sam and I rushed out of the room and down the stairs.

Mom grabbed a basket of goodies she'd put together.

"What did you give Michael and Nicole?" Tori asked me.

I had been so busy feeling sorry for myself that I had forgotten about buying a gift. I stared at the floor and shrugged.

"Don't worry, Piper," Mom said. "The basket is from our whole family to the Austins."

Chief grabbed the car keys off the counter. "Ready, team?"

"Yes, sir!" we said. Then we left the house and climbed into the minivan. The Austins' home in the officers' quarters was a short walk away, but Mom was afraid something might fall out of the basket.

On the way, Tori leaned over to the right so that she could look in the rearview mirror to put on her lip balm and brush her hair a zillion times.

"Tori," Chief said, "you're blocking my view. Please sit back."

When we drove up, I noticed Hailey's and Stanley's families in the Austins' yard. Finally I got to see Stanley's brothers, quiet Kirby and perfect Simon. That explained the goofy way Tori was acting in the minivan. She wanted to impress Simon.

Mrs. Austin had called their going-away

party "a box party," and now I saw why. Stacks of boxes were all over their house. Tomorrow the movers would arrive to pack up the rest of their stuff. "I wish I could ride in the moving van," Michael said. "Then I could sit up high and honk the horn at all the cars we passed."

That would be neat. I wished I could go, too. Seeing all their boxes and hearing Michael talk about the moving truck made me realize Michael and Nicole really were leaving NAS Pensacola. I wished I'd bought them a special gift so that they wouldn't forget me.

Michael's dad cooked hot dogs and hamburgers on the grill and talked to Chief and Stanley's dad.

Tori was sitting at the picnic table across from Simon. She'd been outside five minutes and she already had a bad sunburn. Then I realized the only part of her body that was deep red was her face. Boys always made her blush.

How silly was that? No boy would ever make me turn colors.

I was just thinking how great it was to finally not have to share Michael with anyone except the Gypsy Club when Sam walked over and plopped down between Michael and me.

"What are you doing here?" I asked. I looked over at Kirby, who was sitting by himself, plucking grass blades. "Why don't you go keep Kirby company?"

"He doesn't want to talk," she said.

"Well then, that should work out perfect for you, since you don't want to listen," I told her.

"I can sit anywhere I want," Sam said. "This is a going-away party, and not a Gypsy Club meeting."

"A Gypsy Club meeting can take place any-where," I said.

"Is *that* in the rules?" Stanley asked.

"Yes," Hailey said.

"Of course," I said, turning toward Michael.

"Absolutely," Michael said.

We looked at Nicole.

"I'm not so sure about that," she said.

There were some things that I wouldn't miss about Nicole.

Just then, Brady and his parents arrived. Sam rushed over to them. "Hi, Brady! I'll show you where the chips are." Thank goodness Sam had a three-year-old to boss around so she could stop pestering us.

We ate hot dogs. Then we went inside and watched *The Wizard of Oz* on television. I was kind of glad the movie was on because that way I didn't have to think about the next day. I sure wished I'd given Michael and Nicole something. Hailey gave Michael and Nicole two sets of playing cards. "You'll probably get bored in the car. Norfolk is a long way from here. Maybe you can learn to play canasta."

Stanley gave them a map of Virginia with a red sticker stuck near Virginia Beach.

"What's the marked spot?" Michael asked.

"That's where my grandparents live. On Ventura Street. I didn't want you to get lost when you visited them."

Michael scratched his chin. "Um . . . Stanley, I doubt we'll visit your grandparents."

Stanley stared down at his shoes. "Well, I'm sure gonna miss you when I stay with them in the summer."

Michael punched his shoulder. "Well, why didn't you say so, Stanley? Of course we'll visit your grandparents when you're there."

My hands felt so empty. I tucked them into my pockets. "Our family gave your family a basket of goodies to munch on," I said, embarrassed that I hadn't thought of something super to give them.

"Yummy," Michael said.

"I love goodies," Nicole added. "Thanks, Piper."

But I felt lousy because I really didn't have anything to do with the basket.

I stared at the TV. The Munchkins were on now, and the mayor unrolled a long scroll and gave Dorothy the big welcome. That's when it happened. My incredibly great idea!

5

See You Later

A scroll! I would make a scroll as my gift for Michael and Nicole—a scroll filled with memories. The next morning I got up very early and went to work. The art closet was filled with all kinds of supplies. I found a huge roll of paper in the art closet. There are some benefits of having an art teacher for a mom. I cut a piece of white paper about the length of Sam. Then I took out the colored pencils and began to work.

Every time I thought of something to draw,

I thought of something else. Each idea led me to another one. That's the way ideas are. They multiply. Even the bad ideas weren't really bad because they made me think of a better one.

I drew a picture of my first day at the Blue Angels Elementary School, when Michael showed me he could touch his nose with his tongue. I sketched Nicole flashing her rubber bands and braces. Then I added a picture of our first official meeting and the Gypsy Club Pet Show.

Even though I didn't want to stop working on the scroll, Bruna was sniffing the carpet. I took a break and put her outside to do her business.

Then I went inside and back to work. I had to hurry. The Austins were leaving that morning. I added our Blue Angels field trip, Brady's birthday party, and the Halloween camping trip we'd taken. By the time I'd finished, Chief called out, "Time for breakfast!"

It was Saturday, and that meant pancakes made by Chief, also known as the Pancake Man.

Chief put a stack of pancakes in front of me as Tori and Sam joined us at the table. "You were up early this morning, Piper. What's on your agenda?"

"A surprise for Michael and Nicole."

"A going-away present?" Sam asked.

I nodded and swallowed a bite of pancake. A dribble of blueberry syrup dripped down my chin as I realized Sam was right. This gift was a going-away present. I'd been so busy working and thinking of things to draw on the scroll, I hadn't let it really sink in why I was making it.

I looked at my pancakes. I didn't feel like eating any more. Life wouldn't be the same without Michael and Nicole.

Since Chief was a list maker, we had a list of chores we did every day except for Sunday. (Even Chief believed in a day off.)

This was our Saturday list:

Clear the table: Sam
Wash the dishes: Tori
Dry and put away the dishes: Piper
Walk Bruna: Tori, Piper, and Sam take turns

It was my turn to walk Bruna, so after I put away the dishes and got dressed, I snapped the leash onto her collar. Then I grabbed the scroll and headed toward Michael and Nicole's house. It was ten o'clock in the morning, and they were going to leave at ten thirty.

Tr-ring, tring. I knew Hailey was behind me on her bike without even checking. Sure enough, she rode up to me.

"Hi, Piper! Are you going to Michael and Nicole's house?"

"Yes," I said. For the very last time.

"Beat you there," Hailey said. She took off pedaling like she was racing in the Tour de

France. I watched her red sneakers and spokes
spin until she disappeared around the block.

This was just a taste of what life was going
to be like—Hailey always trying to beat me at
everything I did and top everything I said.

When I reached the Austins' home, Hailey
was talking to Nicole. Stanley was there, too.

Michael was helping his dad carry an ice
chest to their car. He looked up when he saw me

and smiled. I felt like someone had kicked me in the gut. I'd moved all my life. I'd left friends behind everywhere we lived, but I would miss Michael more than anyone.

Nicole waved. "Hi, Piper! Hi, Bruna!"

"Hi, Nicole." She smiled, showing her braces and hot pink rubber bands. I'd miss Nicole, too. She got sick a lot, and she liked to talk about all her allergies, but she was what Mom called a peacemaker. Every club needs a peacemaker.

Stanley walked over to Bruna and patted her head.

Bruna wagged her tail.

"Liver Lump!" Stanley said, grinning.

Bruna barked.

I frowned. "Don't say that, Stanley. I don't have one with me. She'll never stop barking."

Stanley dug in his pocket and pulled out a Liver Lump. "I bought some with my allowance. I don't have a dog, but I figured I'll be seeing

Bruna a lot in the future, especially now that it's just you, me, and Hailey. I'll probably come over every day to keep you company. I could even come over when your dad makes pancakes on Saturday."

"Stanley?" I said.

This time Stanley stopped without me showing him my hand.

"Can we make plans later?" I asked. "Right now I'd like to visit with Nicole and Michael."

Michael wiped the sweat off his forehead with his wrist. "Hey, what do you have there?"

"What?" I looked down at the scroll with the blue ribbon tied around it. I'd almost forgotten. I handed it to him.

"For me?" Michael asked. "Gee, thanks, Piper." He smiled really big.

My face felt hot. I hoped it wasn't red like Tori's got. "It's . . . it's for Nicole, too."

Michael held one end while Nicole gently

took hold of the other. They pulled in oppo-
site directions until the scroll was undone.
Then they stared down at all the pictures that
I'd drawn. They didn't say anything. Hailey and
Stanley moved in closer so they could see. They
didn't say anything either. Even Bruna went
over to them, only she didn't seem so interested
in the picture. She was sniffing Stanley's leg,
probably searching for another Liver Lump.

"I love it, Piper!" Nicole said, "Especially my
purple rubber bands."

Michael studied one of the drawings. "Do I

really look like that when I touch my nose with my tongue?"

Then, all together, we shouted, "Yes!"

Mr. and Mrs. Austin came outside. Mrs. Austin carried her purse, so I knew what that meant. My stomach ached something awful, like I'd swallowed a basketball.

Mrs. Austin hugged each of us. "You've been good friends to the twins," she said. "Let's don't say good-bye. Just see you later."

"See you later," Michael said.

"See you later," said Nicole.

"See you later," Stanley and Hailey said at the same time.

Everyone looked at me, waiting.

I had a big lump in my throat, but I was somehow able to whisper, "See you later." I swallowed hard. That big lump rode down my throat a bit, and I shouted, "Alligator!"

Then I turned away and quickly walked

toward home. Bruna panted as she tried to keep up. Everything looked blurry.

I'm not going to cry. I'm not going to cry. The words played over and over in my head like a chant. The Austins' SUV passed by and sounded three short honks. Michael and Nicole waved. Then they rolled down the window and yelled, "In a while, crocodile!"

I waved back. Stanley and Hailey caught up with me. Together we watched the Austins' SUV drive down the road and turn the corner, disappearing from our sight.

Hailey stared at me. "Are you crying?"

I frowned as I felt a big tear roll down my cheek. "Of course not."

"You look like you're crying," Stanley said.

I wiped my cheek, but it was too late. The tear had already slid off my chin. "It's just allergies."

"Oh," said Stanley. "My brother Kirby has allergies. Especially in the springtime. He——"

"Have a good holiday," Hailey said, rushing away. "Are you going anywhere?"

"To my grandparents' in Piney Woods, Louisiana."

"We're going skiing in Colorado," Hailey said. "My dad rented a condo with a hot tub." She took off, ring-ing her bell as she pedaled. *Tr-ring, tring.*

"I'll walk you home," Stanley said.

"But you live here in the officers' housing."

"Aw, I got all day."

And for the first time ever, I kind of liked Stanley Hampshire walking next to me. It seemed to fill up a little bit of the empty spot inside. Was this what lonely felt like? Or maybe I was just hungry since I didn't finish breakfast.

A few minutes after I got home, Tori said, "Someone is on the phone for you." She held out the receiver to me. I wondered who was calling me. If it was Stanley, he was going to be a big pest.

"Hello?" I said.

"Hey, Piper." It was Michael. Then he asked, "What's your e-mail address?"

6

THE SEARCH FOR ADVENTURE

December was the month for good-byes. The day after telling Michael and Nicole good-bye, we stood in the lobby of the Alexandria Airport, hugging our parents good-bye. The entire way to the airport, Mom had talked about all she wanted to do in Paris—see the Louvre and the Musée d'Orsay, visit the Eiffel Tower, and walk under the Arc de Triomphe. Eat escargots!

"Edie, I'm not eating escargots," Chief said.

"What's escargots?" I asked.

"Snails!" Sam and Tori said together, like I was stupid for not realizing anyone would eat those slimy creatures.

How did they know that anyway? Wasn't it good enough that my sisters were brains in all the American subjects? They also had to be experts in all things French?

"I love taking French at school," Tori said. "It's the most romantic language."

"My teacher taught us foods from around the world," said Sam.

"Oh yeah?" I asked. "What is a food from Spain?"

"Paella!" she said.

I shouldn't have asked. Sam always knew the answers. Only in first grade, and she knew *all* the answers. I didn't ask about another food from another country, but Tori had to rub it in.

"Great, Sam! How about Italy?"

"Gnocchi!" Sam said.

"Poland?" Tori peered at me sideways.

"Borscht." Then she added, "Well, it's technically Russian, but they eat it in Poland, too."

"Okay. Okay," I said. "*So* she knows the foods of every country on the planet. *So* she's smart. *So* what?"

That probably wasn't the best question to ask.

"Being smart is a good thing," Tori said. "Who wants to be dumb?"

Tori didn't say I was dumb, but I knew she was thinking about me when she said that. I had trouble reading because I had dyslexia. Mom was dyslexic, too, and Tori wouldn't dare call her dumb. I hardly thought about being dyslexic. After all, I got to go to Ms. Mitchell's room to read while I sat in her giant beanbag chair. And that made being dyslexic kind of cool.

Our four grandparents met us at the airport before Mom and Chief's flight. We were lucky. A lot of my friends had to go to different cities when they visited all their grandparents. After we said good-bye to Mom and Chief, Grandpa Reed drove our minivan back to his house. That way when Mom and Chief came back, the minivan would be there for us to ride home in.

It would be hard, but the grandmas and grandpas would have to share us. They even made a plan to be fair.

They had strategies.

Grandma Reed flipped through her tiny notebook. "Sam won't eat bananas," she said.

"So I'm not going to waste my time on my delicious banana pudding."

Grandma Morris had a little notebook of her own. "I plan to bake a few dozen cookies for the holidays—pecan sandies are Piper's favorite."

The grandpas didn't bother with notebooks, but they exchanged maneuvers. Grandpa Reed said, "I'm going to change the oil in the minivan. Karl will be too tired to think of it when he gets back from Paris."

"Good idea," said Grandpa Morris. "You might take a look at the condition of the spark plugs, while you're at it."

It was as if the grandmas and grandpas had created their own branch of the military. The plans were to stay at Grandma and Grandpa Morris's the first four days. Then we'd stay at Grandma and Grandpa Reed's house the last four days.

Grandma Morris made us a big pot of chicken and dumplings, which is my very favorite grandma meal. It didn't matter which grandma made it. One bite of the soft dumplings soaking in the broth made me want to jump up and holler, "Get off the bus!"

Uncle Leo came over for dinner. He lived nearby in a little house he bought last summer. When I say little, I really mean *tiny*. When I say tiny, I really mean *teensy weensy*.

"It's ninety-eight square feet," Uncle Leo told us at dinner.

"Does it have a bathroom?" Tori asked.

Bathrooms mattered to my big sister. She was always in the bathroom, trying on makeup (which she is not allowed to wear) and rubbing on thigh thinner cream (which doesn't work).

"Not only does my home have a bathroom," Uncle Leo said, "but it also has a kitchen."

"Could Thumbelina live there?" Sam asked.

Uncle Leo's forehead wrinkled. "Thumbelina? Who is that?"

He didn't know anything about fairy tales. All he knew anything about was hummingbirds. He was a hummingbird expert.

Sam frowned at Uncle Leo when he asked her. "Are you serious?"

"Absolutely," Uncle Leo said. "This is a small town, but I don't know every citizen. Does Thumbelina live in Piney Woods?"

"Everyone knows Thumbelina," Sam said. I could tell from Sam's tone that she thought Uncle Leo was teasing.

Grandma Morris chuckled. "Oh, honey, your uncle Leo doesn't know anything about things such as that. Ask him a hummingbird question, and he'll know the answer."

"Hey, Uncle Leo," I said, "you should name your little house Hummingbird Cottage."

"Well, we really don't get many humming-birds around here," Uncle Leo said.

"Oh, Leo, you are a mess!" said Grandma Morris.

After Uncle Leo left, I asked Grandma, "Can I use your computer?"

"Heavens to Betsy, child, we don't have a computer."

"You don't?" I thought that everyone had a computer.

"No, honey. What on earth would we do with one of those contraptions?"

"Grandma, everyone needs a computer," I said.

"Piper, I'm seventy-five years old, and I've gotten along fine without one for this long."

"But you e-mailed us once," Sam said.

"My friend Bessie Lou did that for me," Grandma Morris said. "It was kind of like a telegram. I called her and told her what to write. Then she called me and told me what you wrote."

"Can we go to Bessie Lou's house?" I asked.

Grandma just peered over her glasses at me.

"I'm sure there is a reason you do need a computer, Grandma," I said, "but I can't think of anything right now."

"You can find coupons for the grocery store online," Sam told her.

Grandma's eyes widened. "Imagine that!"

"And you can look at all kinds of fish." Sam was crazy about fish. She even dreamed of being one.

"Why do you need one now, Piper?" Grandma asked.

"So I can stay in touch with all my friends."

"Won't your friends be on holiday breaks?" Grandma asked. "They could be visiting their grandparents."

"Maybe." Hailey's family was going skiing. Still, I was expecting that e-mail from Michael.

Tori overheard and as usual thought she'd give some bossy advice. "Michael and Nicole just left two days ago. They were going to stop in Alabama to see some relatives. I doubt Michael's had time to e-mail you."

But maybe she was wrong. Maybe there was an e-mail waiting for me, just like there were four adventures waiting for me to discover them.

Since we'd traveled all day and eaten dinner late, we were ready to go to sleep early. Tori got the guest bedroom to herself. Big surprise! Grandpa threw the cushions off the sleeper sofa and unfolded the mattress for Sam and me.

Bruna hopped up on our bed while I got in next to Sam. When Grandma turned out the light, the room became very dark.

"I can't see!" Sam said.

"We're in the country, Sam. Remember, there aren't any streetlights all the way out here," I said. It was kind of eerie though.

"But what if I have to get up and go to the bathroom?" Sam asked.

I hadn't thought about that. "Hey, did you get Annie out of your suitcase?"

Sam gasped. "Oh, my goodness! Grandma, Annie is all alone in my suitcase!"

Grandma heard Sam and flicked on the hall light. Then she brought Annie to Sam, who grabbed the doll and squeezed her tight. It was a good thing that doll wasn't a real baby.

Everyone always looked out for the youngest. What about the middle child who just wants to check her e-mail from her very best friend in the world who has moved to Norfolk, Virginia?

"I'll put a night-light in the bathroom, girls," Grandma said. "That way you can see your way there."

The night light cast a little light from the bathroom into the living room. I could make out everything and everyone.

I thought Grandma had headed to bed, but then I heard her say, "Piper, tomorrow you can walk over to Uncle Leo's house and use his contraption."

"Computer?" I asked.

"Yes," she said. "I'm sure he'll be happy to let you use it."

I think Grandma Morris might be my favorite grandparent.

7

VISIT TO UNCLE LEO'S

Today was my first full day in Piney Woods and a good day for my first great adventure. I didn't know what it would be, but since I planned to have four great adventures, I needed to start right away.

For breakfast, Grandma cooked grits, eggs, and bacon. I wasn't a vegetarian anymore, so that suited me just fine.

Grandpa got up early to go to work at his store, At the Bend in the Road. It was the kind of store that sold snacks, coffee, and gasoline.

I hurried and ate while Sam and Tori slept in. "Can I go to Uncle Leo's?"

"Good gracious, Piper, you don't waste any time, do you?"

"No, ma'am."

"Do you remember how to get to Uncle Leo's? It's in the same place where his trailer used to be."

"Through the gate and at the back of the pasture?"

"Why, yes. That's right. Please remember to shut the gate so that the horses don't get out."

I brushed my teeth and changed clothes. Just as I was about to leave with Bruna, Sam awoke. She rubbed her eyes. "Where are you going?"

"To Uncle Leo's."

"I want to go," she said. "I want to see the Thumbelina house."

"I promise to tell you all about it. Right now I'm in a hurry. Bye." I headed down the hall.

"Piper," Grandma said, "now, you can just wait until your little sister eats and changes. She'd like to go, and she shouldn't go by herself."

Why had I gotten up so early if I couldn't have a few special privileges?

"Would you please feed the cats for me?" Grandma said.

"Sure," I told her.

"Thanks, honey. The cat food is in the shed outside."

"How many cats do you have, Grandma?"

"Gracious, child, I don't know. Sammy might."

"Why don't you know how many you have?"

"Oh, honey, we never did adopt any of those critters. People just drop them off in the country. It's a crying shame, but we don't have a mouse problem. And the vet in the next town over is nice enough to fix them for us so they don't have any kittens."

I decided I would count them. A person should know how many pets they have. Outside I scooped up the food from a huge bag and poured it into three big dishes. When I went outside, there was only one white cat, but after I began to pour the food, three more cats appeared. Grandma and Grandpa had four cats.

How hard is that to figure out? I guess when you get old you forget how to count. I was filling the other three bowls with water when two more cats appeared. Four plus two equals six. Then a calico cat came with six kittens. Six plus seven equals thirteen. Thirteen cats. Thirteen was not a lucky number.

I went back in the house. "Grandma, I thought you said you didn't have any kittens."

"No, honey, I said the vet fixed it where they couldn't have any after they arrived. But that calico gave birth to those kittens the day after she showed up at our place."

"Grandma, you have thirteen cats."

"Oh? Is that all?"

"Yes, Grandma. I counted them. Thirteen cats including the kittens."

"If you say so, dear."

Finally slowpoke Sam finished dressing and brushing her teeth. "I'm ready!"

"Let's go!" I said. "Bye, Grandma!"

"Bye, Grandma!" Sam hollered.

As soon as the front door shut, I shouted, "Beat you there!" I took off running, leaving Sam behind.

"That's not fair," she said. "I'm telling Grandma."

"I can't hear you!" I called out without glancing back.

But I had heard, and I knew Grandma wouldn't be happy with me leaving her behind. So I slowed my pace.

Then Sam slowed her pace.

I tapped my foot. "Hurry up, Sam! I'm waiting for you."

Sam walked even slower.

This was what I got for being a responsible

older sister. If Grandma would have let me, I could have been to Uncle Leo's and back already. Michael was probably wondering why I hadn't answered his e-mail yet. He probably thought he'd lost his best friend in the whole world.

"Sam, I'm taking off if you don't hurry."

Her pace quickened.

I don't know what made me do it. I don't know if it was because I was mad or if it was because I hadn't been able to check my e-mail or if it was because the sun was beating down on my back or if my legs just felt like running. But I took off, racing so fast, faster than I'd ever run in my life. It felt good to sprint across the trail with the pine trees towering above my head, and I forgot all about Michael's e-mail and Uncle Leo's house and Sam until . . .

"Help!"

Turning, I saw Sam lying belly side down on the ground.

I hurried toward her.

"You're in trouble," she said.

I was probably in trouble.

She sat up and pointed to her skinned knees. "You're in *big* trouble!"

I was probably in big trouble.

Fat tears rolled down her cheeks.

I blew on her knees.

"Owwweee, owwweee!" she cried.

I held out my hand to her. "Come on, Sam. We're almost at Uncle Leo's."

She tucked her hands under her armpits. "I don't want your help!"

"I'm sorry. I shouldn't have run off like that."

Sam scowled. "Anything could have happened to me! I could have been kidnapped!"

"Oh, Sam, you aren't going to get kidnapped. There isn't that much distance between Grandma and Grandpa's house and Uncle Leo's."

"You never know."

"Here, let me look at your knees.

"Don't touch them!"

"Okay, okay," I said. "At least let me help you up." I held out my hand again.

This time she took hold of it. "Well, since it is your fault."

I pulled her up.

She hopped on her right foot and then on her left. "Ouch, ouch, ouch! It hurts even more standing."

"Come on. We only have a little way to go. When we get there, Uncle Leo can put some medicine on your knees."

Sam's eyes popped wide. "The *stinging* kind?"

"Gosh, Sam, I don't know. I guess all disinfectants sting."

Sam stopped walking. "I don't want to go."

"If you go back to Grandma's, she'll put disinfectant on it. You might as well get it over with."

I walked very slowly so that I could stay even with her wobbles.

"Ouch, ouch, ouch. The air hurts my knees. Owwww! The sunshine hurts my knees!"

Those were the kinds of times when I tried to ignore Sam. I started to hum "Country Roads," but soon I was singing, "Country roads, take me home to the place I belong . . . Lou-i-si-ana——"

"How can you sing at a time like this? How can you sing when I hurt real bad?"

Then, as if someone had turned off a faucet knob, she stopped crying. Her mouth hung open.

We had arrived at Uncle Leo's cottage. The tiny house, painted red with a yellow door, looked like it belonged in a fairy tale.

"Oh, my goodness," Sam said. "It really does look like a Thumbelina house!"

Sam was right.

She jumped in place three times. "I'm going to pretend Thumbelina lives here, and I'm going to visit her. Maybe we can have a tea party."

I was glad Sam had forgotten about her knees.

She rushed up to the door and knocked. Then she turned around and gave me her "I beat you" look.

Just as Uncle Leo opened the door, Sam burst into tears, pointing down at her knees. "Look at what Piper did to my knees!"

I sighed. "Uncle Leo, I guess we better use your antiseptic and bandages on Sam's knees."

Uncle Leo stared at me like I'd asked for a

platypus and a ferret. "I don't have any anti-septic or bandages."

"You don't even have a first-aid kit?" I asked. Mom and Chief kept first-aid kits at home and in the minivan.

Uncle Leo surveyed his yard as if a first-aid kit might magically fly from behind a bush. "Well, I guess we could take her back to Mother's."

I glanced inside his house and noticed the computer. It was mere inches from me. I wanted to check my e-mail quick so that I could get on with finding my first big adventure. "Do you mind taking her back while I use your computer?"

Sam whimpered. "Ooooh, owwwww!" She might have won a spelling bee, but she'd never win an Academy Award.

Uncle Leo looked down at her. "Maybe I could walk her back."

Sam stretched her arms up to Uncle Leo.
"Don't you think you should carry me?" Sam
asked.

"Oh," Uncle Leo said. Finally, he bent down
and picked her up.

"Thanks, Uncle Leo," I said. "Is there anything I should know about your computer?"

"It's already on. Just minimize my document."

Uncle Leo walked away with Sam's legs
dangling. She glared over
his shoulder at me
and called out,
"This is all
your fault!"

8

YOU'VE GOT MAIL

Uncle Leo's cottage didn't have a bed anywhere in sight. Just a desk and chair on one wall and a stove, microwave, and small refrigerator on the other. Where did Uncle Leo sleep?

I plopped down in front of the computer and stared at Uncle Leo's document. He sure knew a lot of big words. A lot of big, boring words. I minimized the document and looked for the Internet browser. I didn't recognize it, so I started opening every icon on the screen.

There was one about the eating habits of hummingbirds and another about the migration patterns of hummingbirds. Each of the icons had something to do with hummingbirds. No browser anywhere.

I decided to wait for Uncle Leo. I walked around his cottage, which was a little like spinning in place. It took about three seconds. Then I noticed a latch on one of the walls. What a funny place for a latch. I wondered what it was for. I ran my finger over it. Then I slipped my finger under the latch and the wall started to fall. I jumped back just as the wall landed with a *thump!* Magically, a bed appeared.

The front door opened, and Uncle Leo froze in the entrance. "Were you planning to take a nap?"

"Sorry, Uncle Leo. Did I break it?"

Uncle Leo lifted the end of the bed and pushed it against the wall before latching it in

place. "You didn't break it. It's a Murphy bed."

"Oh." I glanced back at the computer. "Uh, Uncle Leo, I couldn't find the browser."

"The browser?"

"To get on the Internet."

Uncle Leo nodded. "Oh." Then he said, "I don't have Internet service."

"You don't? Why didn't you tell me?"

"You said you needed to use the computer. You didn't say you needed to use the Internet."

I had forgotten. Uncle Leo might be a genius, but we had to explain everything exactly or we might as well be speaking Polish. Uncle Leo's head was so filled with hummingbirds, he didn't have time to think about anything else.

"Don't you ever need the Internet?" I asked.

"Not often. When I do, I go to the library."

"Can we go to the library?"

"I guess we could go as soon as I finish this article," he said.

"When will that be?" I asked.

Uncle Leo scratched his head. "Oh . . . some-time in February."

"Uncle Leo, it's December. I won't be here in February."

Uncle Leo looked at me with his blank stare.

I could see I was going to have to take charge. Lucky for me, I was used to that since

I'd started two Gypsy Clubs. "How about after lunch today?"

"Well . . ."

"Uncle Leo, I'm expecting an important e-mail."

"Well . . ."

"See you after lunch, Uncle Leo. Why don't you pick me up in front of Grandma and Grandpa's house at one o'clock?"

"Well, I . . ."

"Bye, Uncle Leo! See you at one o'clock. Sharp!"

Back in Grandma's kitchen, Sam shot mean, dirty looks at me the entire time that I ate my sandwich.

"I hope your face isn't going to freeze like that," I told her.

"Why are you eating so fast?" Tori asked me.

"Uncle Leo's taking me to the library. I'm going to check my e-mail."

"I want to go," Tori said, wiping her mouth.

"I might have some e-mail waiting for me."

"I doubt Simon will have time to write you. He'll be too busy winning a contest or a race or running for president."

"I'm going, and you can't stop me."

"Me, too." Sam jumped to her feet. A Big Bird bandage covered each knee.

"What happened to the injured person?" I asked.

"Grandma made it better."

I worried that Uncle Leo would forget or at least arrive late, but at one o'clock sharp he drove up in front of the house and tapped on the horn.

"Bye, Grandma!" We whizzed by her and dashed out the front door.

Uncle Leo drove to the library. We climbed out of the car, but he didn't move.

"Aren't you coming inside?" I asked.

"No," he said. "I don't need to go to the library."

Tori bent over so that her face was even with his. "We won't take long."

Inside, Sam rushed over to the children's section and started pulling books off the shelf.

"Sam," Tori said, "don't pull too many books off the shelf. We're only going to be a little while."

Then we got permission from the librarian to use the Internet. She wrote the day's password on a piece of paper, and we headed toward the computers.

I had one e-mail message. From Stanley. It was a long e-mail. He told me everything he had done, including brushing and flossing his teeth. Then he told me everything Simon had done—surfing in Hawaii with his friend's family.

Tori didn't have an e-mail from Simon, just

her friend Josie. I could tell because I peeked over her shoulder. She sighed.

"I guess you didn't hear from Simon, since he went surfing in Hawaii."

"How do you know that?" she asked.

"Stanley e-mailed me."

"Can I read it?"

"Okay." What did I care? It wasn't like the e-mail was from Michael.

I had to wait for her to read the entire e-mail. After she finished, she said, "I'll bet Stanley has never had a cavity."

We logged off and helped Sam reshelve the books before we left the library. We stared at the parking lot. Uncle Leo was nowhere to be found.

"Maybe he went to the post office," I said.

"Or the bank," Sam said.

Twenty minutes later, Tori asked, "Piper,

when you asked Uncle Leo to take us to the library, did you tell him we needed a ride back?"

"No," I said.

We were stranded in the parking lot at the Piney Woods Public Library.

"I guess we better call Grandma," I said.

Tori nodded. "Good thinking, genius!"

9

~~~

ADVENTURE ONE
The Store Around the Bend

The day was almost over, and I hadn't had an adventure or gotten an e-mail from Michael. Maybe he'd lost my address. He had a lot to think about while he was moving. Why hadn't I asked Michael for his e-mail? Or maybe he meant he'd e-mail a few months from now. Or maybe he'd already made new friends and forgotten about me.

Before bedtime that night, Grandpa said, "Chuck went home sick today." Chuck was

Grandpa's bag boy. "Who wants to work at the store with me tomorrow?"

"I will!" I said.

"Pick me," Sam said.

Tori stared out the window. No surprise— she was allergic to work. If Grandpa had ever seen Tori's bedroom, he would never ask her to help. Tori Reed was the messiest person on the base. She dropped clothes all over her room, even though she had a walk-in closet. It was a good thing she wasn't in the military. She would never pass inspection.

"I'll do it, Grandpa," Sam said. "I could help little kids pick out candy."

"There's more to being a bagger than choosing between M&M's and Twizzlers," I told her.

"I'm afraid Piper is right, Sam," Grandpa said. "It's hard work. Piper, you're hired. You'll need to get up before dawn."

"Yes, sir!" I said. Grandpa Morris is my favorite grandparent.

Sam poked her lips out until Grandma said, "Sam, I could sure use some help feeding."

"Feeding who?" Sam asked.

"Feeding Tori," I said. "That's a full-time job."

Tori snapped her head in my direction. "Piper Reed, you're mean!"

Grandma ignored us and said, "Well, there's lots of feeding to do—the chickens, the cats, Dewy, and Stella." Dewy was the donkey, and Stella was their old dog that didn't want to do anything but sleep.

Sam bit her nail and then put her finger near her temple. She did that every time she was thinking hard about something, as if it helped her find the answer quicker. A second later she announced, "Okay!"

The next morning I awoke from someone gently touching my shoulder. "Time to get up, bag girl," Grandma said.

Today I was going to have my first big adventure. I slipped into the bedroom where Tori was sleeping. As I searched through the drawer for my clothes, Tori said, "Can you *please* get dressed quietly? Some people are trying to sleep."

"You're just jealous because I get to work at Grandpa's store," I said. Secretly I was glad she hadn't volunteered. If she had, Grandpa probably would have chosen her to go instead, since she was the oldest.

"No regrets here." Then Tori pulled the sheet over her head. Doing something is always more fun when someone else wants to do it.

"I'm going to have a great adventure today," I said.

Tori's head popped out from under the cover. She peered at me through tiny slits.

"A great adventure? Bagging groceries? Stocking shelves? Sorry—that's not the kind of adventure I'd have in mind."

Tori Reed was not going to make me feel like I'd made the wrong decision. "I guess you're in charge of Bruna, then." I swung her door wide open. "Here, Bruna. Come here, Bruna."

Bruna appeared, but she looked sleepy, leaning forward into a stretch.

"You can start right now," I told Tori. "She needs to go outside." Then I took off for the kitchen.

Grandma cooked a breakfast of fried eggs and bacon for Grandpa and me. Then Grandpa and I left to start our day at the store.

It was still dark outside when Grandpa unlocked the front door and turned on the lights. "Piper, I'm going to make some coffee. Would you turn the sign in the window around and then water the camellias?"

I flipped the sign so that it said OPEN. Then I hurried outside and used the hose to water the camellias.

A pickup truck filled with giant bags of pecans drove up. "Hello, Sammy," said the man in the truck.

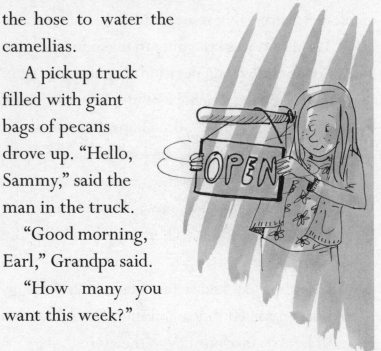

"Good morning, Earl," Grandpa said.

"How many you want this week?"

Grandpa rubbed his chin. "How about thirty?"

The man went to the back of the truck and started handing bags to Grandpa and me. We stacked them outside next to the wall.

By the time we finished unloading the pecans, a delivery truck had driven up and dropped off three boxes.

"What's in the boxes?" I asked Grandpa.

"Chips," Grandpa said. "From the distribution center."

"Distribution center?"

"The distribution center buys from the companies, and I buy them from the distributors."

Grandpa Morris's grocery store was a lot more complicated than I'd thought, but I didn't know how anything today would turn into a big adventure. Tori was right. And I hated when she was right.

Before the sun was up, we had about eight customers. None of them needed a bag. They just wanted coffee or a doughnut.

"Those are my early birds," Grandpa said.

I dusted and stocked shelves. I stared out the window and noticed a huge convertible heading toward the store, but it wasn't slowing down.

"Grandpa, I think that car is going to hit your store!"

Grandpa barely glanced out the window. "Oh, that's Mrs. Shepler. She can brake that tank on a dime."

Sure enough, Mrs. Shepler screeched to a stop inches from the door. Then she sat there in her car.

"She's waiting for Chuck to open the door for her. Could you do that, Piper?"

I dashed outside and opened her car door.

Mrs. Shepler peered up from under her white hat. Her brown eyes glared at me through her

spotty glasses. "What did you do to your hair, Chuck?"

"I'm not Chuck," I said. "I'm Piper Reed."

"Piper Reed. Are you related to that boy Karl Reed?"

"My dad is named Karl Reed, but he's a chief in the U.S. Navy."

"Is that where that boy went off to? I haven't seen him in years."

I'd forgotten that Chief used to work at Grandpa's store. I had the same job as my dad.

"Aren't you going to get out of the car?" I asked her.

"Hold on," she said. "I'm not a spring chicken."

Mrs. Shepler grabbed her purse from the passenger seat and snapped it open. With white-gloved hands, she dug in and pulled out a tube of lipstick. Then she twisted the rearview mirror so that she could put it on. I thought she was through when she dropped the tube back into her purse, but then she dug inside until she pulled out a wrinkled tissue and dabbed her lips.

"I'm ready," she said, offering her hand.

I took hold of it and gently tugged.

Mrs. Shepler rocked back and forth. She

scowled at me and said, "You're going to have to pull harder than that."

I yanked with all my might until I fell flat on my back.

Mrs. Shepler didn't fall, though. She'd released my hand and was standing over me. "What on earth are you doing down there?"

"Nothing."

"That boy Karl Reed used to count clouds, too."

Then I brushed myself off and hurried to the front door so I could open it for her.

Mrs. Shepler took itty-bitty steps toward the entrance.

Inside the store, I helped her find every item on her list, bagged her groceries, and helped her back into the car. I was exhausted.

When she started her car, I said, "Grandpa, I don't think Mrs. Shepler should drive."

Grandpa kept putting the napkins in the holder. "Oh, she'll be all right."

"I mean it, Grandpa. She's probably danger-ous behind the wheel."

Grandpa closed the napkin holder and motioned me over to the window. When I met him there, he pointed to a yellow house next door. "See that house?"

"Yes, sir."

"That's where Mrs. Shepler lives." He winked at me, smiling. "She doesn't even have to pull onto the road. She just drives on the dirt shoulder between the store and her house. And, by the way, she should need you right about now."

"Sir?"

"She'll need you to unpack the groceries and put them in her pantry."

I raced out the door and reached the house just as Mrs. Shepler parked her car. *This* was no great adventure. After I finished helping her, she opened her purse. "Here," she said. "This is a little something for you."

She held out a shiny nickel. Mrs. Shepler must have thought she was tipping during Chief's time as a bag boy. She stood there smirking like she was waiting for me to say something.

"Oh," I said, "thank you."

"You're welcome."

About an hour before Grandpa closed the store, a black limo drove up. A chauffeur got out and opened the back door. "What in tarnation?" Grandpa said.

Out stepped a young woman with long blond hair and dark sunglasses. "She looks familiar," I said.

"She's not from these here parts," said Grandpa.

Then I knew. It was Margie Marcel, Tori's favorite actress. Why was a movie star in Piney Woods, Louisiana?

She walked into the store barefoot.

Grandpa stared at her bare feet. "Excuse me, ma'am." Grandpa pointed to the sign. NO SHOES, NO SHIRT, NO SERVICE.

"Okay," she said. "Ralph, could you grab my shoes?"

"You're Margie Marcel," I told her.

"Yes," she said. "I am."

Ralph handed her her shoes. She dropped them and slipped them on.

"Where are the Twinkies?" she asked.

I ran and got her a package. Then she grabbed six packs of peppermint gum. She undid four pieces and stuck them in her mouth.

"Do you want me to bag those for you?" I asked.

She glanced down at the small package of Twinkies. "Sure, why not?"

Grandpa only had large bags, but I dropped the Twinkies into the bag anyway and tossed in the gum.

"Ralph, give the cute kid a tip."

Ralph opened up his wallet and gave me a twenty-dollar bill! That made up for Mrs. Shepler's shiny nickel.

"Get off the bus! Thanks!" Maybe Margie Marcel was my favorite actress after all.

"No problem."

"Do you mind giving me your autograph?"

"Sure. Just one, okay? We're in a hurry to get to New Orleans."

Grandpa tore a page out of his tablet. He handed it to her along with a pen.

Finally my first great adventure in Piney Woods—a real movie star was talking to me, and now she was giving me her autograph!

"How do you spell your name?" she asked.

I started to speak, but then I paused.

She peered at me over her sunglasses. "Kid? How do you spell it?"

I opened my mouth and said, "T-o-r-i."

10

~~~

ADVENTURE TWO
SURVIVING THE SLEEPING PORCH

When I gave Tori the autograph, her mouth flew open. No words came out. She didn't even say thank you. But she stared at that autograph until bedtime.

The next morning, Tori decided she wanted to go to work with Grandpa. She thought Margie might show up at the store again. I thought one Margie Marcel sighting in Piney Woods was about as much as you could hope for.

"I'm glad you want to work, Tori," Grandpa

said. "I could use both of you to help with the inventory."

Didn't Grandpa know about Tori's work allergy? She'd only had one job—babysitting the Milton triplets—and she failed at that.

We worked the rest of the week at the store. We counted candy, chips, and soda. If Grandpa's store carried it, we counted it. I didn't care if I ever counted again in my life. Margie Marcel didn't drop back in, but Grandpa paid us forty dollars each. I should have gotten more since I worked an extra day, but Grandpa was getting old. He probably forgot how to do math.

Uncle Leo took us to the library the night before the big switch. This time he waited while we checked our e-mail. I had two from Stanley, one from Hailey. None from Michael or Nicole.

Mom and Chief sent us an e-mail through Tori's e-mail address. They said they missed us, but they were enjoying walking around Paris and drinking coffee in the cafés. That sounded boring to me, but Tori sighed like Mom and Chief had told us they'd eaten a huge chocolate cream pie.

The night of the big switch, we packed our bags and Grandpa and Grandma Morris drove us over to Grandpa and Grandma Reed's house. We had to drive through the town of Piney Woods and turn on a road that wove through thick, piney woods.

When we rode up to their little blue house with a tin roof, Sam said, "Grandma and

Grandpa Reed live in a little house in the big woods, just like my book." She'd started reading the Laura Ingalls Wilder books this year and she was already halfway through the series.

Grandpa Reed met us outside. "Y'all are staying for supper, aren't you?" he asked our other grandparents.

"Oh, we don't want to impose on you," Grandma Morris said.

"It's no trouble at all. Mertie is making her fried chicken and potato salad."

"Well, since it's fried chicken," Grandpa Morris said, "I think we'll stay."

Grandma Morris shook her head. "Oh, Sammy, where are your manners?"

"Why is that bad manners?" I asked. "Grandpa Reed asked you to stay."

A few minutes later the seven of us squeezed around the kitchen table to eat Grandma Reed's famous fried chicken and potato salad.

"We're lucky," I said.

"Why is that?" asked Tori. She was still sore about not getting to see her favorite movie star.

"We get to have our grandparents all together."

"What do you mean?" asked Sam.

"All my friends have to go to different cities and sometimes states to see both of their grandparents. We get to eat fried chicken at the same table with ours."

Tori rolled her eyes like I had said something dumb, but Grandma Reed said, "Well, Piper, that's smart and kind of you to appreciate that."

"Yes, indeed," Grandma Morris said. "Very thoughtful, Piper."

"I'm glad we don't have any more grandparents all together, though," Sam said.

"Why?" I asked.

"Because then we couldn't have an extra piece of chicken."

The grandparents laughed.

"Could you pass the chicken please?" Sam asked.

"Baby, you can have all the chicken you want," said Grandma Reed. "And if we run out of chicken, I'll just have Charlie go into the hen yard and catch one. Then I'll wring another neck for you."

"Nobody can wring a chicken neck like you, Momma," Grandpa Reed said.

Suddenly I wasn't hungry. Sometimes having grandparents who live in the country can make you reconsider being a vegetarian.

After our grandparents left, Grandma Reed said, "The weather has been warm enough, y'all can sleep on the porch if you want."

"Get off the bus!" I loved sleeping on the back porch. Usually we only got to do that during our summer visits.

"And your cousins will be here this week," Grandma said. "The hayride is on Christmas Eve, too. Uncle Seth will be pulling a trailer with his tractor like he does every year."

Sam and I dressed into our pajamas and plopped onto the roll-away bed on the porch. Grandma Reed had piled an extra feather mattress and four quilts on top, making the bed extra soft and tall.

Sam squealed and pulled the top quilt up to

her chin. "I'm the princess and the pea!"

"Sam," I said, "why do you have to turn everything into a fairy tale?"

She sat straight up. "That's not what my new story is about. Do you want to hear it?"

"No," I said, rolling over on my side so I couldn't see her.

Tori and Grandma walked onto the porch.

After Tori crawled into bed, Grandma said, "I'll tuck you in."

When Mom or Chief said they'd tuck us in, they just meant they'd come into our room and say good night. But Grandma really meant it. She tucked in the sheets and all the quilts between the mattresses.

"There you go," Grandma said when she finished. "Snug as a bug!"

Then she gave each of us a mushy grandma peck on our cheeks. "Good night!"

"Sleep tight!" we said.

"Don't let the bedbugs bite!" Grandma said. Then she turned out the lights.

As soon as the light flicked off, the porch turned totally dark. It must have been a cloudy night because I couldn't see the stars, and only a sliver of the moon was showing. I held up my hand in front of my face. I couldn't see it. I wiggled my fingers. I couldn't see them either.

"I'm not scared," Sam said like she was trying to convince herself.

"How about a scary story?" Tori asked.

Tori's stories were never scary, not even on Halloween night.

"Okay!" Sam said.

"Sure," I said. Now I'd be asleep in no time.

"There was an old lady with a hatchet," Tori began. She made her voice creak. It didn't sound like her at all. Suddenly a picture of Grandma Reed holding a hatchet flashed in my mind. Only she didn't look nice and cozy like

Grandma. She looked like a mean and scary version of her. Maybe it was because of what she said about wringing the chicken's neck at dinner.

Tori continued. "The old woman liked to use her hatchet on *everything*."

I closed my eyes, but I could see chickens running around the yard, running away from Grandma and her hatchet.

"Oh, my goodness," Sam said. "This is like an adventure."

This was one adventure I didn't want.

Tori's story caused the creepy crawlies to travel up my spine. I tried not to listen. I tried to think of our cousins who would arrive soon.

"Everyone was afraid of the old woman," Tori said, "with her squeaky knees, bony fingers, and shiny hatchet."

"Oooooh," Sam said. She stuck her cold feet on my legs.

I jumped out of bed. "I need to go to the bathroom."

Thump! "Oowooo!"

"Sorry, Bruna!"

I'd accidentally caused Bruna to fall out of bed, and then I stepped on her.

"I'll wait until you get back from the bathroom to finish," Tori said.

"That's okay," I told her.

With my hands out in front of me, I quickly felt my way toward the door. Suddenly, I touched something soft.

"That's my belly, cricket," a creaky voice said.

I screamed.

"Piper, it's just me—Grandma."

I screamed again. "D-d-do you have a hatchet?"

"A hatchet?"

Tori laughed.

"I was just kidding," I said, trying to sound brave. "I was trying to scare Sam."

"I'm not scared!" Sam said. "It's only a story."

"Just checking to see how you girls were doing," Grandma said.

After I went to the bathroom, I noticed Grandma had turned on a night-light in the hallway.

When I got to bed, Tori was sound asleep. I was glad she was through with her story. Then a dog from far off began to howl. Dogs from all over joined in. Normally it wouldn't bother me to hear dogs howling, but sleeping on the porch when the sky was pitch-black and knowing

there might be an old lady with a hatchet walking around took dog howling to a whole new
level.

I tossed and turned, but I couldn't fall asleep.
The night in Piney Woods was filled with howls
and creaks and wind moaning.

"Sam, are you asleep?" I asked.

"Mm-hmm," she said in a dreamlike state.

"Sam, I can't go to sleep because I'm too
excited thinking about your new story."

"Oh!" Sam seemed awake now.

I hated asking, but I had no choice. "Could
you please tell me all about it?"

"My pleasure," Sam said. "Once upon a time,
a princess visited a little house in the big woods."

It was going to be a long night.

11

COUNTING COUSINS

"**W**hich cousins are coming?" I asked Grandma Reed at breakfast.

"Each and every precious one," Grandma Reed said, checking the other side of the pancake.

"Oh, too bad Megan can't come," I said. There was nothing precious about Megan.

Grandma peered at me. "*All* of my grandchildren are precious to me."

Drats. That mean ole Megan was coming.

"How many cousins are there now?" Sam asked.

"Well, let's see," Grandma said. "Uncle Riley and Aunt Lynette have Megan and Collin."

"That's two," I said.

"Five," said Sam. "There's three of us."

Smarty-pants Sam. If she didn't watch out, she was going to grow up to be just like Megan.

Tori came to the table. She stretched her arms over her head.

"Good morning, Victoria," Grandma Reed said.

"A good morning doesn't start until noon," Tori said.

There was no hope for Tori. She was already like Megan. Maybe worse because I had to live with Tori.

"We're not done counting cousins yet," Sam said.

I nudged Tori. "We're taking inventory."

Tori groaned.

Grandma Reed flipped a pancake high in the air and caught it with the skillet. I guess Grandma was the reason Chief was the Pancake Man. "That's right, Sam. Let's see, back to the cousins. Uncle Seth doesn't have any."

"Zero plus five equals five," Sam said.

"That's right, Einstein," I said.

"Why are we counting cousins?" Tori asked, rubbing her eyes.

"Because they're all going to arrive tomorrow morning," I told her.

"Which means I need to go to the grocery store," Grandma said. She slid three pancakes on a plate and gave them to me.

"Hey," Sam said, "I didn't get mine yet."

"Yours are coming up, Sam," Grandma said. "Piper was at the table first."

Sam was used to being first at so many things  because she was the youngest. Tori was the first at other things because she was the oldest. But at Grandma Reed's table, the middle child ruled. I shouldn't pick favorites, but Grandma Reed is my favorite grandparent.

"We're still counting," Sam said, eyeing my pancakes.

I slowly spread butter on each one, then drizzled a lot of syrup over the stack. I cut a small piece, slipped it into my mouth, then smiled at Sam as I slowly chewed.

"Oh, there's Cousin Ginger Bee," Sam said, "but she's only three."

"She's still our cousin," I said.

"That makes six."

"Aunt Ladybug has Twyla and Spider." Grandma poured some more batter in the skillet. It made a sizzling sound.

Tori was wide awake now. "Is there any reason our family names their children after insects?"

"They're nicknames," I said. Even I knew people didn't go around naming their kids after eight-legged creatures.

"I know," Tori said, "but most people have more ordinary nicknames."

"Where's the fun in that?" Grandma Reed asked.

Sam jumped and yelled, "Eight! There are eight cousins!"

"You win a million dollars," I told her, before taking a big gulp of milk.

Sam ignored me. "You can do a lot of things with eight people."

"Oh, boy!" Tori clapped her hands together. "We could have our own rodeo!"

Tori didn't mean it, but I didn't care.

Something exciting was going to happen. My next great adventure.

"Get off the bus!" I shouted. "Great idea, Tori! A cousin rodeo!"

My mind buzzed with the rodeo idea. When Grandma announced that she was going to town to the grocery store, I asked if I could ride over with her and go to the library.

I checked my e-mails. There were none from Michael or even from Stanley, but there was one from Mom and Chief. They'd sent a couple of pictures in an attachment. One was of them standing in front of the Eiffel Tower. The other was of Mom studying a van Gogh painting at the Musée d'Orsay. They were smiling, but I figured they were pretending so that we wouldn't realize how sad they were without us.

The next morning I recruited Tori and Sam

to help gather the stuff we needed for the rodeo.

"We need rope," I told Tori.

"Rope? What on earth for?" she asked.

"Have you ever seen a rodeo without rope?"

Sam was getting into the spirit of the rodeo, though. "Can we use the chickens in the rodeo?"

I thought about it a second. Then I said, "I've never seen chickens in a rodeo. But I have an idea. We could have a chicken parade at the beginning of the rodeo."

Grandpa Reed and Uncle Seth hung the bucking barrel to four pine trees that grew close to each other. Four lengths of rope attached at one end to eyehooks in the barrel, and the other ends were tied tightly around the tree trunks. Another, longer piece of rope was tied around the barrel.

Uncle Seth threw a small saddle on the barrel. "This used to be my bucking barrel in my rodeo days."

"You were in a rodeo?" I asked. "What did you do?"

"Rode bulls," Uncle Seth said, glancing sideways at Grandpa Reed.

Grandpa Reed chuckled. "Fell off bulls is more like it."

Uncle Seth's face turned red.

"That's okay, Uncle Seth," I said. "I've never known a rodeo bull rider before."

Uncle Seth dug his boot heel into the dirt. "Well, it's not like I was a champion or anything."

"How does the bucking barrel work?" I asked.

"Hop up," Uncle Seth said.

Uncle Seth bent over with his hands cupped like a stirrup. I stepped onto his palms and climbed atop, straddling the barrel. Grandpa Reed took hold of one of the back ropes and Uncle Seth grabbed hold of the other.

"Hang on, cowgirl," Grandpa Reed said.

I grasped the center rope. "Ready!"

Grandpa Reed and Uncle Seth yanked on the ropes, causing the barrel to buck. They pulled, and I held on.

"Yeehaw!" I yelled, holding my right arm high in the air. "Look at me, Tori!"

Tori barely glanced up from writing in her poetry notebook. "Yippee." She might as well have said "big deal."

I knew who would be impressed. "Look at me, Sam!"

Sam ran over. "Wow! I want a turn."

Now we had four events for the rodeo—the chicken parade, barrel racing with Buster (after my wild ride on Buster the last time we visited, I decided to sit this one out), the bucking barrel, and lassoing the fence post.

All afternoon, I practiced and practiced throwing the rope over the fence post. I got pretty good at it. I figured, why settle for a fence? Maybe I would surprise everybody the next day by lassoing Martina, the milk cow.

12

ADVENTURE THREE
THE COUSIN RODEO

At ten o'clock, Megan and Collin arrived. They lived down the road from Grandma and Grandpa Morris and had been on vacation in New Orleans. Then Aunt Sarah and Uncle Buck arrived with Ginger Bee. Sam quickly took over Ginger Bee like she was her own personal project.

"Now, Ginger Bee," she told her, "you can be in the chicken parade, but you're too young for barrel racing, the bucking barrel, and lassoing."

"I want to lass-o," Ginger Bee said, pouting.

"She can lasso," I said. What would it hurt? A three-year-old couldn't throw it hard enough to get hurt.

"Okay," Sam said. "I guess you can lasso, Ginger Bee."

"Good," Ginger Bee said. Then a second later she asked, "What's lass-o-zing?"

Collin and I were practicing on the bucking barrel when Aunt Ladybug drove up with Twyla and Spider.

"Guess what?" I told them. "You're going to be in the Cousin Rodeo."

If I had learned anything from my Gypsy Club events, it was that a successful event takes a lot of planning. If I learned anything from the Cousin Rodeo, it was that one day is not enough for planning.

During the chicken parade, Sam and Ginger

Bee walked in front of the chickens, tossing feed like flower girls in a wedding dropping petals. The rest of us walked on the sides and in the back to keep the chickens in line. The chickens followed closely. A little too closely for Ginger Bee, who thought they were trying to peck her. She began to scream and run. "Oooo, those chickens are trying to kill me!"

This upset the chickens, and they scrambled about, flapping their wings and chattering nervously. Feathers flew as we ran around trying to gather the birds.

The bucking barrel event came just in time. Uncle Seth yanked on the ropes while we took turns riding the barrel. Only he didn't yank too hard, and everyone got bored watching each rider hold on f-o-r-e-v-e-r.

"Looks like our family is made up of champion bucking barrel riders," I said.

"Well, we're no Ty Murrays," Spider said.

"Ty Murray?"

The other cousins gasped. "You don't know who Ty Murray is?" said Megan. "He's just a world-champion bull rider."

"Can't believe you didn't know who he was!"

"Well," I said, "I didn't know you meant *that* Ty Murray."

Next was the barrel racing event. Earlier I'd helped Uncle Seth and Grandpa place five barrels in the pasture. The racers would be timed as they rode Buster around the barrels. The rider with the quickest time would win.

"Aren't you going to ride Buster?" Collin asked me.

"I'm resting up my lassoing arm."

"Are you sure it doesn't have to do with the last time you rode Buster?" Megan asked.

Tori laughed. "It has everything to do with her last ride on Buster."

I ignored them, but they were right. Buster was an adventure I didn't want to repeat.

Grandpa Reed overheard and said, "Now, I'll have you know, once you ride a getaway horse and the saddle goes south side on ya, that qualifies the rider as a genuine trick rider. And that *dis*qualifies them from competing against non-professionals."

"Really?" Collin asked.

"Wow!" said the other cousins. (Except for Megan, who rolled her eyes along with Tori.)

"Yes, sirree," Grandpa Reed said.

I loved Grandpa Reed. Without a doubt, he was my favorite grandparent.

I watched as my cousins took turns riding Buster and knocking down barrel after barrel. Sam decided she'd sit out the event, too.

"Who do you think will win?" Sam asked.

"Probably Collin," I said. He rode horses more than any of us.

I was wrong. Collin rode around the barrels, kicking his heels into Buster's side. The harder he kicked, the slower Buster went, knocking down the last barrel before finishing.

His time: three minutes and twenty-seven seconds.

"Stupid Shetland," Collin said, hopping off Buster. "I can go more than twice that fast on my horse."

Then it was Tori's turn. She put her left foot in the stirrup and pulled herself up, holding the saddle horn. Before she could swing her right leg over the saddle, Buster took off running, ignoring all the barrels.

"Aaaaah!" Tori yelled as she held on, leaning over the saddle with one foot still in the stirrup.

Uncle Seth chased after them and grabbed the harness. For a few seconds, he had to run beside them to keep up. "Whoa!" he said.

"Aaaaah!" Tori yelled.

"Whoa! Whoa!"

Finally Buster stopped. He stopped so quickly that Uncle Seth fell on one side of him and Tori fell on the other.

Tori quickly got up and brushed herself off. Her face was redder than I'd ever seen. Even redder than the times she saw a boy she liked.

From the fence, I hollered, "Hey, Tori, I guess this makes you a genuine trick rider, too!"

Tori's hands rolled into fists. She looked like she wanted to punch me.

"Lasso time!" I yelled. I couldn't wait to show off my new skills.

We let Ginger Bee go first. She merely picked up the rope and tossed it in the air above her head. It landed inches from her toes. Ginger Bee stared down at the rope. "I don't want to lass-o-zing no more." Then she marched over to Grandma Reed.

I volunteered to go last because lassoing Martina would be the big finale. I watched cousin after cousin throw the rope. Spider was the best one. He roped the fence post three times out of his five chances.

Then it was my turn. I picked up the rope and turned away from the fence post, focusing on Martina the milk cow. Her calf was a few feet away, but when I swung the rope in Martina's direction, the calf went toward the mother and the lasso slipped over *her* head instead.

Get off the bus! No one knew I was aiming

at Martina. They probably thought I was focusing on the calf. I waited for the applause, but I only heard some gasps. Maybe they were waiting for me to bow. So I bent low, still holding on to the rope.

Sam yelled, "Watch out, Piper!"

I straightened. Then I felt a tug.

"Uh-oh," I said. The calf ran off, dragging me around the pasture. Martina didn't look too happy with the rope around her baby, and she started chasing me. I guess she thought I was chasing her baby. My feet tried to keep up. The calf kicked up a lot of dirt. I opened my mouth to scream but swallowed the dirt instead. I felt the scream rising from my throat, but all I could manage was "Hic-cup! Hic-cup . . . hic-cup." How could a person get the hiccups at a time like this? The closer Martina got to me, the faster my hiccups came.

"Drop the rope, Piper!" yelled Tori.

I dropped the rope and headed toward the fence. Then I climbed over and fell on the other side just before Martina reached me.

The cousins ran over and looked down at me.

"Hic-cup!" I waited for Megan to make fun of me. Instead she bent over and held out her hand. "That was awesome, Piper!"

I grabbed hold of her hand, and she gave it a yank, pulling me to my knees.

"Yeah, Piper," Spider said. "You're pretty good at that lassoing."

Then all the cousins and my sisters yelled, "Get off the bus, Piper Reed!" And just like that, my hiccups were gone.

That night we crawled to the top of the hay stacked on Uncle Seth's long trailer for the hay-ride. We stopped at homes along the road and

sang carols. Every house we stopped at, people came out and passed around cookies or hot cocoa or just gave us good wishes. Our holiday was almost over, and there'd only been three adventures, but the Cousin Rodeo with the hayride finale was the best one of all.

13

~~~

ADVENTURE FOUR
AN UNEXPECTED ADVENTURE

The cousins went home, and we crawled into bed on the screened porch.

"Will Santa really know we're here in Piney Woods?" Sam asked.

"Of course," Tori said. "Santa knows where everyone is on Christmas Eve. What do you want Santa to bring you for Christmas, Sam?"

"He knows," Sam said. Then she closed her eyes. Mom and Dad always told us Santa wouldn't come unless we were asleep.

"What do you want for Christmas, Tori?" I asked.

Tori smiled and said, "I already received my best Christmas present—a genuine Margie Marcel autograph." She paused, then added, "Thank you, Piper."

I felt sparkly like a Christmas tree with a hundred lights flashing.

Sam opened her eyes, "We forgot something."

"I know what it is," I said. "Tori?"

Tori read *Cajun Night Before Christmas*. Her accent was pretty good, and I listened to every word. After she finished, I felt so sleepy. On Christmas Eve, it usually takes us hours to fall asleep, but that night on our grandparents' porch, we raced off to dreamland.

The next morning, I awoke when the sun was rising above the chicken house and the rooster was crowing. I lay there for a minute thinking about how much fun we'd had the day before. If only Mom and Chief could have seen me lasso that calf.

"I don't think barrel racing is my sport," Tori whispered. "Every bone in my body aches."

Sam opened her eyes wide. "It's Christmas!"

"We need to wait until seven-thirty. Remember what Mom and Dad said?"

"What time is it?" I asked.

"Seven," called a voice from the kitchen. It was a familiar voice. But it wasn't Grandma Reed's.

"That's more like oh-seven hundred."

I looked at Tori and Sam, who looked as surprised as me.

"Is this a dream?" Sam asked.

I pinched her.

"Ouch."

"No," I said. "It's not."

All three of us ran into the kitchen and into Mom's and Chief's arms.

"We took an earlier flight. We couldn't stand the thought of being without our three girls on Christmas Day," Mom said.

"Especially," Chief said, "since I missed last Christmas while I was on ship duty."

I knew they missed us.

We didn't even look under the tree because the very best present was standing right in front of us. Sometimes you don't have to seek out an adventure. Sometimes the adventure comes to you.

And that was the best adventure ever. At least, that's what I thought until we got home.

When we arrived back at the base, Stanley was waiting by our door.

"Hi, Stanley," I said. I didn't know until that minute, but I had kind of missed him. Bruna had, too. She raced over to Stanley and barked.

"Hi, Piper. Hey, Bruna. Guess what I have for you?" Stanley reached in his pocket and pulled out a Liver Lump. After he gave it to her, he asked me, "Did you get a letter from Michael and Nicole?"

"No, did you?"

"Yes," he said. Then he took a big breath like he was getting warmed up to rattle on and on.

I didn't wait for Stanley to say another word. I rushed next door and got our mail from Yolanda and Abe. And there in the stack of bills and cards was a letter addressed to me.

Dear Piper,

   We don't have Internet service yet, so we wanted to write you a letter because we miss you and the other Gypsies.

   Norfolk is really cool. You should see the shipyard. It's huge, and they decorated all the ships with lights for the holidays. Maybe you can visit us sometime. Until then, we promise to start another Gypsy Club.

Your pals,

Michael and Nicole

P.S. We have now spread "get off the bus" to the state of Virginia!

That night, Chief told us he had a surprise. He would tell us after midnight in the new year.

"Is it an adventure?" I asked.

Chief looked over to Mom. She smiled and nodded.

"You could say that," he said.

I guess if you think about it, adventures are always around the corner, just waiting to be discovered.

Later, we watched the ball fall at Times Square, and when they did the countdown, we yelled together, "Ten, nine, eight, seven, six, five, four, three, two, one!"

Instead of saying Happy New Year, I asked, "What's the surprise?"

"We have our new orders. We're moving."

"What?" squealed Tori who always hated to move from one place but then always fell in love with the next place. We'd lived in Pensacola for only a little over a year. Usually we stayed somewhere at least two years.

"Where are we moving?" I asked.

"Norfolk, Virginia," Chief said.

"Norfolk, Virginia?" I couldn't believe my luck. "Get off the bus!"

That was the biggest adventure ever. And it hadn't even happened yet.

Go Fish!

GOFISH

Kimberly Willis Holt

© Shannon Holt

Are Tori, Piper, and Sam Reed based on your own family growing up?
Yes. Although most of the book comes from my imagination, the setup is very autobiographical. My dad was a Navy chief and I am one of three girls. However, I'm the oldest. Growing up, I was the serious one, the bossy one, the one who worried about her weight. I didn't think that point of view would be as interesting as my middle sister's. She was the funny one, the confident one, the clever one.

Being the middle sister has its advantages and disadvantages, but ultimately Piper seems stronger as a result of her position in the family. Do you agree?
I do. All the sisters are planners, but Piper has the most guts. She's not afraid to speak her mind and she does what

she sets out to do. She doesn't always get the results she hoped for, but she goes for it.

As a child, you lived on many different Navy bases because your father was stationed all over the world. What did you like most and least about being a Navy brat?

I don't think I truly appreciated what a military life offered me while I was growing up. I hated moving. I was shy and didn't make friends easily. About the time I would start to feel at home, we moved, again. Now I look back on that experience and realize how rich a childhood I had. I was exposed to many cultures. And I learned to be adaptable and tolerant. I'm interested in people. Even though I was shy growing up, now I feel like I can talk to anyone. I believe that is because of my childhood.

What are some of the ways in which the life of a Navy family is different today than it was back when you were growing up?

One major difference is that when the parents are away on an assignment, military kids today can stay in touch with them more easily. I interviewed several groups of Navy kids whose parents were serving on a ship. They told me how they e-mailed their mom or dad every day. A couple of kids even played Internet games with their military parent. Now that's a huge improvement. I can remember when my dad was away we looked forward to the mail—snail mail.

Another difference is that there are a lot of kids with moms serving in the military today. That wasn't common when I was a kid. That's why I wrote about two of Piper's friends having their moms serve on the same ship as Piper's dad.

Is there really such a thing as Sister Magic?
Sure. I think it really has to do more with shared life experiences than genes, though. My sisters and I might laugh at something that no one else would think was funny.

When did you realize you wanted to be a writer?
In seventh grade, three teachers encouraged my writing. That was when I first thought the dream could come true. Before that, I didn't think I could be a writer because I wasn't a great student and I read slowly.

What's your first childhood memory?
Buying an orange Dreamcicle from the ice-cream man. I was two years old.

What's your most embarrassing childhood memory?
In fourth grade, I tried impressing the popular girls that I wanted to be friends with by doing somersaults in front of them. (I never learned to do cartwheels.) They called me a showoff, so I guess it didn't work. If only I'd known how to do a cartwheel.

What was your first job?
I was in the movies. I popped popcorn at the Westside Cinemas.

How did you celebrate publishing your first book?
I'm sure my family went out to dinner. We always celebrate by eating.

Where do you write your books?
I write several places—a big soft chair in my bedroom, at a table on my screen porch, or at coffee shops.

Where do you find inspiration for your writing?
Most of the inspirations for my writing come from moments in my childhood.

Which of your characters is most like you?
I'm a bit like most of them. However, I fashioned Tori in the Piper Reed books after me. But Tori is bossier than I was and she certainly makes better grades than I did.

What's your idea of the best meal ever?
That's a toss-up. My grandmother's chicken and dumplings, and sushi.

Which do you like better: cats or dogs?
I'm a dog person. I have a poodle named Bronte who is the model for Bruna.

Who is your favorite fictional character?
Leroy in *Mister and Me* because he is forgiving. And that's a trait many of us don't have.

What's the best advice you have ever received about writing?
A writer once told me, "Readers either see what they read or hear what they read. Writers have to learn to write for both." When I started following that advice, my writing improved.

What do you want readers to remember about your books?
The characters. I want them to seem like real people. I want them to miss them and wonder what happened to them.

What would you do if you ever stopped writing?
I plan on dying with a pen in my hand.

What do you wish you could do better?
I wish I could do a cartwheel.

What would your readers be most surprised to learn about you?
I send gift cards with positive messages to myself when I order something for me.

Navy brat Piper Reed is moving again. This means she has to say good-bye to all the friends she's made in Florida, including the Gypsy Club. But when Piper meets a new friend, Arizona, she thinks she may have found her best friend yet!

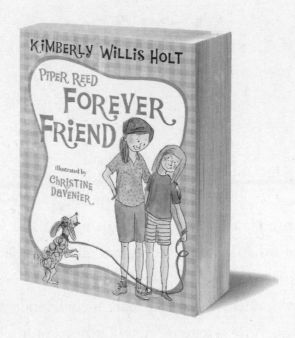

Turn the page to read an excerpt from

PIPER REED FOREVER FRIEND

by Kimberly Willis Holt.

1

A Fish Tale

In December, Chief got his new orders from the U.S. Navy. We were moving to Norfolk, Virginia. I'd be saying good-bye to the Gypsy Club that I started here, but since Michael and his twin sister, Nicole, had moved to Norfolk last month, I already had two friends there. Enough for a new Gypsy Club. I couldn't wait for my new adventure to begin.

When we moved to Pensacola, Florida, fifteen months ago, there'd been five of us—

Chief, Mom, my sisters Tori and Sam, and me. Now two more had joined our family—our dog, Bruna, and Sam's goldfish, Peaches the Second.

Bruna would be moving with us, but not Peaches the Second. Sam pitched a big fit when Chief broke the news. "That's not fair! Just because Peaches the Second is a fish?"

"Sam, just think about it," I said. "This is what it would be like for Peaches the Second trapped in a plastic bag on a long car ride." I sucked in my cheeks and crossed my eyes. Then I rocked side to side.

Even Tori glanced
up from her poetry
book and laughed.
And she hardly ever
cracked up at any-
thing I did. I guess
thirteen-year-olds
don't have a sense of humor. At least I
had three years to go before I lost mine.

Chief patted the spot next to him on the
couch. "Come here, Sam."

Sam plopped near him, but crossed her arms
over her chest. "But, Daddy, what's going to
happen to Peaches the Second?"

I placed my hands over my heart,
trying to look sad like someone at
a funeral. "Most goldfish eventu-
ally experience the great flush
in the sky," I said.

"The what?" Sam asked.

My fingers flushed an imaginary commode handle in the air, and I said, "*Ker-plunk!*"

Sam burst into tears.

Tori slammed her book shut. "Piper Reed, you are mean!"

"Piper," Chief said, "you aren't helping matters." He wrapped his arm around Sam and said, "Sweetheart, the drive would be too long for Peaches."

"Peaches the Second," Sam corrected him.

Chief hit his forehead with a flat palm. "Of

course, Peaches the Second." Then he winked at me. "Yes, she could . . . uh . . ."

I began to sing the only funeral song I could remember. "In the sweet by and by . . ."

Chief lowered his eyebrows at me just as Mom walked into the room with a laundry basket.

"Why don't you give Peaches the Second to Brady?" I asked.

"That's a great idea, Piper," Mom said. "Brady loves Peaches."

"THE SECOND!" Sam yelled.

Mom sighed. She was sorting through the laundry, tossing the unmatched socks into a pile. Chief kept a sack of unmatched socks and tried to match them up each time he did laundry. He called it the Single Sock Looking for Love Sack. Mom ignored the sack and threw them into her art bag for sock puppets or some other art class project.

When Tori had found out, she'd said, "Mom's and Dad's sock systems totally contradict each other."

"Yep," I'd said, "and that's why the Reed family goes around sockless most of the time."

Then Mom pitched one of my favorite socks in her art project pile, the one with jets all over it.

"Wait!" I dashed across the room and rescued it. Once the sock was safe in my hands, I asked Sam, "So what do you think about giving her to Brady?"

"But I don't want to give Peaches the Second to him," Sam whined. "Then I won't have a fish." She puckered up her lips and started that pretend cry she used whenever she couldn't get the tears to come.

Chief stood up and headed toward the kitchen. "Sam, if you give your fish to Brady, we'll buy you a new one when we get to Norfolk."

Sam wiped her phony tears with her shirttail. "How about two?"

The pantry door squeaked open, and Chief pulled out a loaf of bread. "Okay, two goldfish."

Sam should be a lawyer. She knew how to get Chief to cave in. He was at his weakest when he was hungry.

"Everyone grab a plate," Chief called out. "I'm making tuna fish salad sandwiches for dinner tonight."

"What?" Sam squealed. "How could you?"

"Chief didn't say goldfish sandwiches." A picture of Peaches the Second flopping between two pieces of rye bread flashed in my mind, and I started laughing.

"What's so funny?" Sam asked.

"Nothing," I said. "It's kind of a private joke."

Tori chuckled. "That sounds fishy."

Even I cracked up. That was the first time in her entire life my big sister, Tori Reed, said anything funny.

JOIN IN THE FUN AND READ ALL THE
PIPER REED BOOKS
BY KIMBERLY WILLIS HOLT AND
ILLUSTRATED BY CHRISTINE DAVENIER

Book 1: PIPER REED, NAVY BRAT

978-0-312-62548-1

Book 2: PIPER REED, CLUBHOUSE QUEEN

978-0-312-61676-2

Book 3: PIPER REED, PARTY PLANNER

978-0-312-61677-9

Book 4: PIPER REED, CAMPFIRE GIRL

978-0-312-67482-3

Book 5: PIPER REED, RODEO STAR

978-1-250-00409-3

Book 6: PIPER REED, FOREVER FRIEND

978-0-8050-9008-6

SQUARE FISH

MACKIDS.COM
AVAILABLE WHEREVER BOOKS ARE SOLD